P9-EDL-968

No longer
the Property of the
Seattle Public Library

The Bee

Published by Inhabit Media Inc.
www.inhabitmedia.com

Inhabit Media Inc. (Iqaluit) P.O. Box 11125, Iqaluit, Nunavut, X0A 1H0
(Toronto) 191 Eglinton Avenue East, Suite 301, Toronto, Ontario, M4P 1K1

Design and layout copyright © 2021 Inhabit Media Inc.
Text copyright © 2021 by By Becky Han
Illustrations by Tindur Peturs copyright © 2021 Inhabit Media Inc.

Editors: Neil Christopher and Kelly Ward
Art Directors: Danny Christopher and Astrid Arijanto

All rights reserved. The use of any part of this publication reproduced, transmitted in any form
or by any means, electronic, mechanical, photocopying, recording, or otherwise, or stored in a
retrievable system, without written consent of the publisher, is an infringement of copyright law.

We acknowledge the support of the Canada Council for the Arts for our publishing program.

This project was made possible in part by the Government of Canada.

ISBN: 978-1-77227-300-7

Library and Archives Canada Cataloguing in Publication

Title: The bee / by Becky Han ; illustrated by Tindur Peturs.
Names: Han, Becky, author. | Peturs, Tindur, illustrator.
Identifiers: Canadiana 2021021483X | ISBN 9781772273007 (hardcover)
Subjects: LCGFT: Picture books.
Classification: LCC PS8615.A548 B44 2021 | DDC jC813/.6—dc23

Printed in Canada

The Bee

By Becky Han · Illustrated by Tindur Peturs

I was happy being outdoors
with nothing to worry about.

3

Then I heard something that startled me, you see.

I knelt down and prayed, "Please help me!"

And then I heard, "*Apita, bzzz, bzzz, bzzz.*"

5

Qaariaq, qaariaq, qaariaq. Oh, that darn bee.

Qaariaq, qaariaq, qaariaq!

I started crying, "Qaariaq, qaariaq, qaariaq."

I started running really fast. There I went, *poof*!
I kept running for three whole days and ended up in a different community.

I asked, "Where am I?" and someone replied, "*Aak!* Igloolik."

While I was resting, I was startled once again, and I heard,

"*Apita, wait for me! Bzzz, bzzz, bzzz.*"

Qaariaq, qaariaq, qaariaq. That darn bee.

Qaariaq, qaariaq, qaariaq!

I started crying, "Qaariaq, qaariaq, qaariaq."

I started running really fast. There I went, *poof*! I kept running for five whole days and ended up in another community.

I asked, "Where am I?" and someone replied, "*Mailuaq!*

Rankin Inlet."

While I was resting, I was startled once again, and I heard, *"Apita,*

I won't hurt you!"

And I replied . . .

"Hey, Bumblebee, *bzzz, bzzz, bzzz,* come here, come here, come here, dear little bee. Come here, come here, come here. I'm not afraid of you!"

"Come here, come here, come here! We'll play together outside all day."

Pronunciation Guide

Notes on Inuktitut Pronunciation

There are some sounds in Inuktitut that may be unfamiliar to English speakers. The pronunciations below convey those sounds in the following ways:

· A double vowel (e.g., aa, ee) lengthens the vowel sound.

· Capitalized letters denote the emphasis for each word.

· q is a "uvular" sound, a sound that comes from the very back of the throat. This is distinct from the sound for k, which is the same as a typical English "k" sound (known as a "velar" sound).

Term	Pronunciation	Meaning
Apita	A-pee-ta	name
qaariaq	QAA-ri-aq	saying meaning, "Don't come near me."
aak	AAK	exclamation meaning, "Here!"
mailuaq	MAI-lu-aq	exclamation meaning, "It's too much."

For more Inuktitut-language resources, visit inhabitmedia.com/inuitnipingit.

Becky Han is an Inuk singer-songwriter who grew up in the small and beautiful community of Ikpiarjuk (Arctic Bay) in Nunavut. Believing that music is a creative and educational outlet, she enjoys writing most of her work in Inuktitut. *The Bee* is based on her award-winning song "Qaariaq."

Tindur Peturs is an animator and illustrator, born and raised in Iceland, who moved to Canada to study animation and Canadian culture. They have a love for nature, animals, and the power of storytelling.

Iqaluit · Toronto